A SPECIAL WITCHES' BREW

Written By: Andy Rector
Illustrated By: Norma Garris

"Look, Bozwell," Winnifred Witch said to her cat. "They're coming up on the porch!" Winnifred Witch looked forward all year to greeting the trick-or-treaters who would visit them throughout the evening on Halloween night.

Winnifred was a happy little witch. She wanted to make friends with the other children in the neighborhood, but they were afraid of Winnifred's sisters, Sassy and Fussy.

"Sisters!" said Winnifred. "Are the goodies ready?"

Sassie and Fussie brought out a witches' brew for the trick-or-treaters to drink.

"We've been working all day," said Sassie.

"Yes," said Fussie. "We hope the little kiddies will like it." Then Sassie and Fussie looked at each other and winked.

Winnifred knew her sisters were going to play a mean trick on someone. They did it every year.

"Well," said Winnifred, "your punch will go nicely with the chocolate chip cookies I made for the trick-or-treaters."

"I'm sure they will," said Fussie. Then Fussie and Sassie looked at each other again and smirked.

Winnifred saw the smirk and worried that someone was going to have a trick played on them that night.

Ring! went the doorbell.

Winnifred hurried to answer the door. "Trick or treat!" yelled the visitors.

"Hi, everybody!" said Winnifred. "We have chocolate chip cookies and punch for you tonight."

Winnifred handed out her cookies and poured punch for everyone. When the boys and girls ate the cookies they said "Yummy" and "These are good." But when they drank the punch, they began to make faces.

"This punch tastes awful," said a trick-or-treater.

"Who made this punch anyway?" asked a boy in a devil costume.

"We're never coming back here again," they said. The trick-or-treaters grabbed their masks and loot bags and ran away from Winnifred's house.

Winnifred felt sad. Tears began to well up in her eyes. "Now I'll never make friends with the other children in the neighborhood," she said to herself. Then she heard her sisters laughing.

"The punch was the mean trick you were going to play on people this year," she said to them.

"Of course it is!" said Sassie.

"We're witches," said Fussie. "We're suppose to do mean things!"

Winnifred ran to the back of the porch and cried. Bozwell rubbed up against her and purred.

"Oh, Bozwell," Winnifred said with a sniffle. "Why do they have to be so mean. I'm trying to make friends with other children, but I won't be able to if my sisters are going to play mean tricks on them every Halloween.

"I should have made my own witches' brew," said Winnifred. "That's it. I WILL make my own witches' brew. Only this time it won't taste awful."

Winnifred ran out into the garden with a flashlight and found some Giggleberries and Snickerroots.

Then Winnifred ran into the kitchen pantry to find some Grin Juice and her Grannie's cookbook.

"Let's see," she said to herself. "What else can I use in my special witches' brew?" She found the recipe for Happy Brew in her Grannie's cookbook.

"I still need Hee-haw Spice and Chuckle Sauce to make Happy Brew." Then Winnifred looked around the pantry some more and found some Hee-haw Spice and Chuckle Sauce.

Winnifred used the recipe for Happy Brew from her Grannie's cookbook. She mixed twelve Giggleberries, a teaspoon of Snickerroots, a cup of Grin Juice, a dash of Hee-haw Spice, and a teaspoon of Chuckle Sauce all together in her little cauldron.

"This brew," thought Winnifred, "is going to make everyone smile." After a few minutes she announced, "It's done! My Happy Brew is done!"

"Here, Bozwell," Winnifred said, "Tell me what you think." She poured some of her Happy Brew into Bozwell's drinking dish.

Bozwell ran over to his bowl. Winnifred saw his little red tongue lap up some of her happy juice. After a few seconds Bozwell grinned and began rolling around on his back. He purred so loudly that Winnifred was sure her sisters could near it in the next room.

"It works!" said Winnifred stroking Bozwell's fur. "I've never seen Bozwell so happy before!"

Winnifred took her Happy Brew to the streets. "Happy Brew anyone?" Winnifred asked Trick-or-Treaters. "Won't you have some of my Happy Brew?"

"I like your witch costume," said a little girl dressed as a fairy princess.

"Thank you," said Winnifred. "Would you like some Happy Brew?"

"That sounds good," said the fairy princess.

Winnifred poured the princess a cup of Happy Brew.

The princess swallowed a gulp of Happy Brew.

"This is really good!" said the Princess with a giggle. "It makes me want to laugh and laugh and laugh." And that's what the little girl did. She laughed and laughed and laughed as she walked away.

Winnifred saw some trick-or-treaters sneaking around her house. They were the same ones who tasted Sassie and Fussie's nasty punch. Winnifred saw them holding things in their hands. They were eggs.

"They're going to throw eggs at my house!" she thought. She ran over to them. "Why do you want to throw eggs at my house?" asked Winnifred. "Because you tricked us," said a boy dressed like a devil. "You gave us yucky punch."

"That was my sisters' punch," explained Winnifred. "Why don't you try my Happy Brew?"

"How do we know this isn't another trick?" one of them asked.

"If you don't like this punch," said Winnifred, "Then you may go ahead and throw eggs at my house."

"Okay," they said.

She lifted her jug and poured some Happy Brew for them to drink.

Soon they were all drinking Happy Brew and smiling. Then they grinned. Then they snickered. Then they laughed out loud. Then they began howling with laughter.

"We love your Happy Brew, Winnifred," they said. They laid their eggs down. They didn't feel like playing tricks anymore.

"What is this laughing?" yelled Sassie sticking her head out a window.

"Come out and see for yourself," yelled the children.

"Why are all these children laughing?" Fussie and Sassie asked each other. "Our punch is supposed to make people unhappy and mean."

HA! HA! HA!

They stepped outside and stood in front of Winnifred.

"We heard all the laughter," said Fussie. "What is going on out here?"

"This made them happy," said Winnifred, holding up her jug of Happy Brew.

"Let me see that," Sassie said and grabbed the jug from Winnifred. She took a big swallow and handed it to Fussie. Fussie drank some, too.

"What's so special about this . . .?" Sassie said. Suddenly she started giggling. Then Fussie started laughing. They made such a noise laughing that all the kids in the neighborhood came running back to Winnifred's yard.

"Where did you get this recipe," said Sassie.

"Yes, tell us," said Fussie. "It's delicious."

"I found the recipe in Grannie's cookbook," said Winnifred. "I made Grannie's Happy Brew."

"Good for you!" said Winnifred's sisters.

"I have an idea!" said Winnifred. She told everyone what she had in mind.

Everyone gathered in Winnifred's backyard. She gave Happy Brew to everyone who came by for treats. Sassie and Fussie gave them rides on their magic brooms.

That Halloween, Winnifred made lots of new friends in the neighborhood because no one was afraid of her sisters anymore.